DOCTOR · WHO

THE CULT OF SKARO

BBC CHILDREN'S BOOKS
Published by the Penguin Group
Penguin Books Ltd, 80 Strand, London, WC2R 0RL, England
Penguin Group (USA), Inc., 375 Hudson Street, New York, New York 10014, USA
Penguin Books (Australia) Ltd, 250 Camberwell Road, Camberwell, Victoria 3124, Australia.
(A division of Pearson Australia Group Pty Ltd)
Canada, India, New Zealand, South Africa.
Published by BBC Children's Books, 2007
Text and design © Children's Character Books, 2007
Images © BBC 2004
Written by Matt Kemp. Birth of a Legend by Justin Richards
10 9 8 7 6 5 4 3 2

Printed in China.
ISBN-13: 978-1-40590-312-7
ISBN-10: 1-40590-312-0

CONTENTS

MEET THE CULT OF SKARO

When the Great Time War with the Time Lords seemed inevitable, the Dalek Emperor set up The Cult of Skaro — a secret order of four Daleks whose job was to think the unthinkable and to dare to imagine. It was a plan so incredible that the Cult of Skaro became a myth — not even the Doctor was sure they really existed.

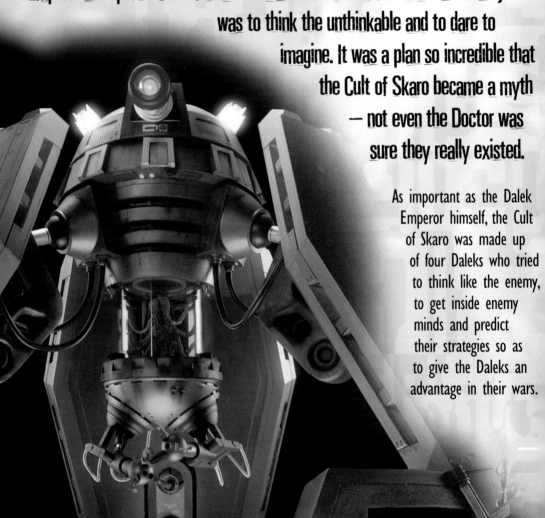

As important as the Dalek Emperor himself, the Cult of Skaro was made up of four Daleks who tried to think like the enemy, to get inside enemy minds and predict their strategies so as to give the Daleks an advantage in their wars.

The Daleks in the Cult of Skaro even had names.
They were called Thay, Sec, Jast, and Caan. They
looked just like other Daleks — hideous mutated
creatures living inside their armoured shells. Only
Dalek Sec — leader of the Cult of Skaro was
different. Sec had a distinctive black casing.

Their mission was to ensure the survival of
the Dalek race at any cost, and they managed
to survive the Great Time War. But even
the other Daleks did not realize how far
Dalek Sec was prepared to go to preserve
the Daleks.

Name:	Dalek Sec
Title:	Leader of the Cult of Skaro
Height:	1.68m (5'6")
Home Planet:	Skaro (destroyed in the Great Time War)
Construction:	Metalert-enforced Dalekanium
Special abilities:	Mind-reading
Mode of transport:	Void ship/Temporal Shift
Mission:	To ensure the survival of the Dalek race

DALEK SEC HYBRID ANATOMY

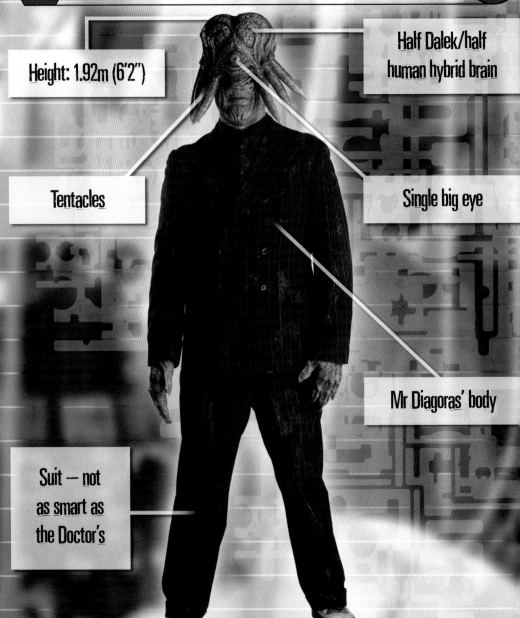

Height: 1.92m (6'2")

Half Dalek/half human hybrid brain

Tentacles

Single big eye

Mr Diagoras' body

Suit — not as smart as the Doctor's

1. WHICH WAR DID THE CULT
   OF SKARO SURVIVE?
   A. World War II
   B. The Great Time War
   C. The War of the Worlds

2. HOW MANY DALEKS MAKE UP
   THE CULT OF SKARO?
   A. Three
   B. Five
   C. Four

3. WHO IS DALEK SEC?
   A. Leader of the Free World
   B. Leader of the Cult of Skaro
   C. Leader of the Pack

4. WHAT IS THE CULT'S
   PRIMARY MISSION?
   A. To find new civilizations
   B. To protect the Dalek Emperor
   C. To ensure the survival of
      the Daleks

5. WHAT DOES THE HUMAN
   DALEK HYBRID WEAR?
   A. A battered old suit
   B. Tracksuit bottoms and a hoodie
   C. A floppy hat and a long scarf

TEST YOUR KNOWLEDGE

EMPEROR DALEK

The Cult of Skaro was set up by the Emperor Dalek and was allowed to carry out its work independent of the Emperor. While the Cult of Skaro devised a plan to make sure they survived the Great Time War, the Emperor led the Dalek armies against the Time Lords. Despite the millions of casualties on both sides, the Emperor survived, and slowly built up a new army of Daleks by converting humans kidnapped from a space station — the Game Station. But the Emperor did not know that he and his army were not the only Dalek survivors...

THE DALEKS

With the Emperor destroyed, it seemed as if the Daleks of the Cult of Skaro were the only Daleks still in existence. But they had rescued thousands of Dalek prisoners from the Time War, in the Time Lord prison they called the Genesis Ark.

These Daleks were released over London and joined the battle against the Cybermen over Canary Wharf. But they were sucked into the Void between universes by the Doctor and Rose.

After their escape to New York in 1930, the Cult of Skaro were forced to adopt a different plan to create more Daleks.

MR DIAGORAS

Believing themselves to be the last four Daleks in existence, the Cult of Skaro planned to evolve the Dalek race by bonding human and Dalek flesh.

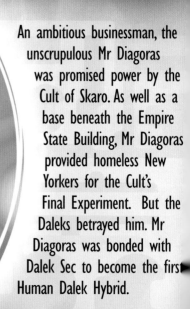

An ambitious businessman, the unscrupulous Mr Diagoras was promised power by the Cult of Skaro. As well as a base beneath the Empire State Building, Mr Diagoras provided homeless New Yorkers for the Cult's Final Experiment. But the Daleks betrayed him. Mr Diagoras was bonded with Dalek Sec to become the first Human Dalek Hybrid.

PIG SLAVES

The Cult of Skaro created an army of Pig Slaves out of homeless New Yorkers who were not considered clever enough to be used in the Final Experiment. Vicious and unthinking, the pig-faced creatures were trained to capture more humans, and to help the Daleks as they planned their Final Experiment.

Because of the way they were created, the Pig Slaves only lived for a few weeks — which suited their Dalek masters.

1. WHO DESTROYED THE EMPEROR DALEK?
   A. Rose Tyler
   B. Martha Jones
   C. The Doctor

2. WHAT WAS THE NAME OF THE CULT'S PROJECT?
   A. The Human Slave Scheme
   B. The Final Experiment
   C. Mission Impossible

3. WHICH TWO CITIES DID THE CULT OF SKARO TRY TO TAKE OVER?
   A. New York and Berlin
   B. New York and London
   C. London and Cardiff

4. WHAT AMERICAN LANDMARK WAS MR DIAGORAS IN CHARGE OF?
   A. The Empire State Building
   B. The Statue of Liberty
   C. The Chrysler Building

5. HOW LONG DO PIG SLAVES LIVE?
   A. About three days
   B. About three months
   C. About three weeks

TEST YOUR KNOWLEDGE

THE DOCTOR

The Doctor is the last of the Time Lords — the race that the Daleks fought in the Great Time War. He is their greatest enemy and has defeated them in many times and places. Every time he thinks he has won, they find a way to re-group and build an army once more. He lost his companion Rose in his last battle against the Cult of Skaro, and this made him even more determined to rid the universe of the Dalek threat.

The Doctor managed to prevent the Dalek's succeeding with their Final Experiment and the Daleks themselves destroyed the hybrid race they had created. But one Dalek, Dalek Caan, escaped. And he's out there, somewhere in the universe. Waiting and plotting against the Doctor.

MARTHA JONES

Training to become a doctor, Martha Jones was more than a little surprised when her whole hospital was transported to the moon. But then she met the Doctor — and together they stood up to the alien Judoon and an evil Plasmavore.

In awe of the Time Lord, she managed to convince the lone traveller to take her "on the scenic route" back to her own time — with various exciting, and sometimes frightening, detours along the way. An intelligent woman, she is determined to prove herself to the Doctor. Her common sense and medical knowledge make her an ideal companion for the renegade Time Lord.

TALLULAH AND LASZLO

Laszlo was a stagehand at the Laurenzi Theatre when he was taken to the Daleks. He managed to escape before the process of turning him into a Pig Slave was completed, and returned to the theatre to see the woman he loved, Tallulah — a singer and dancer.

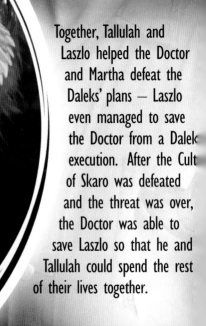

Together, Tallulah and Laszlo helped the Doctor and Martha defeat the Daleks' plans — Laszlo even managed to save the Doctor from a Dalek execution. After the Cult of Skaro was defeated and the threat was over, the Doctor was able to save Laszlo so that he and Tallulah could spend the rest of their lives together.

THE CYBERMEN

"Inferior species", "crude cybernetic constructs" — there's no doubt that the Cult of Skaro have little respect for their robotic enemies, the Cybermen. Despite both being ancient enemies of the Doctor, until recently, they had never encountered each other. The Battle of Canary Wharf saw the Daleks fight the Cybermen for the first time but there was only ever going to be one winner — the Doctor. Both races were sucked into the Void between universes, with only the Cult of Skaro managing to escape.

1. WHO DID THE DOCTOR LOSE FIGHTING THE CULT OF SKARO?
A. K-9
B. Sarah Jane
C. Rose Tyler

2. WHAT WAS MARTHA JONES' JOB ON EARTH?
A. School teacher
B. Trainee doctor
C. Actress

3. WHERE DOES TALLULAH WORK?
A. The Laurenzi Theatre
B. The Globe
C. Tamworth Assembly Rooms

4. WHO CAPTURED LASZLO?
A. The Cybermen
B. The Pig Slaves
C. Dalek Caan

5. WHAT DID DALEK SEC CALL THE CYBERMEN?
A. "An inferior species"
B. "Jolly nice metal people"
C. "Hovering tin cans"

TEST YOUR KNOWLEDGE

ORIGINS

The Cult of Skaro was set up by the Dalek Emperor as a secret order designed to think as their enemies think and devise new ways of keeping the Dalek race alive. The Emperor chose four Daleks to form the Cult, each of which had proven themselves to be outstanding in their fields - a Force Leader, a Commandant of a research facility, an Attack Squad Leader and a Commander.

The Dalek home planet, Skaro, was destroyed in the Great Time War, but the Cult of Skaro survived. The Doctor discovered that their fundamental DNA type is 467-989, but beyond that details of the mysterious Cult of Skaro are few and far between.

THE GREAT TIME WAR

The Daleks discovered that, long ago, the Time Lords of the planet Gallifrey had tried to prevent the Daleks ever existing. The Time Lords had sent the Doctor back in time to stop them being created. When they found out, the Daleks retaliated, and a full-scale war erupted within the Time Vortex and beyond that in the Ultimate Void.

Hiding in the Void between universes as the war raged, the Cult of Skaro waited and planned. They had with them a captured Time Lord prison — the Genesis Ark. When the Doctor defeated the Daleks who emerged from the Genesis Ark, the Daleks of the Cult of Skaro managed to escape using an emergency temporal shift to travel in time.

SURVIVORS

The shift took them to 1930's New York, where they devised their most horrifying plan yet. With only four Daleks left, they had to find a way to ensure the future of their race. They created a way to bond with the very species that they have tried to destroy countless times - the human race. The Doctor managed to stop them once more, and destroy three members of the Cult. But the Dalek threat continues, as Dalek Caan survived.

1. WHAT IS THE CULT'S DNA TYPE?
A. 467-989
B. 210-771
C. 191-106

2. WHICH OF THESE IS NOT ONE
   OF THE CULT OF SKARO?
A. Jast
B. Caan
C. Rabe

3. HOW DID THE CULT FLEE
   THE GREAT TIME WAR?
A. In a Void Ship
B. In the Genesis Ark
C. In the TARDIS

4. WHAT DECADE DID THE CULT
   TRANSPORT THEMSELVES INTO?
A. 1920s
B. 1930s
C. 1940s

5. HOW MANY OF THE CULT
   SURVIVED TO LEAVE NEW YORK?
A. One
B. Two
C. Three

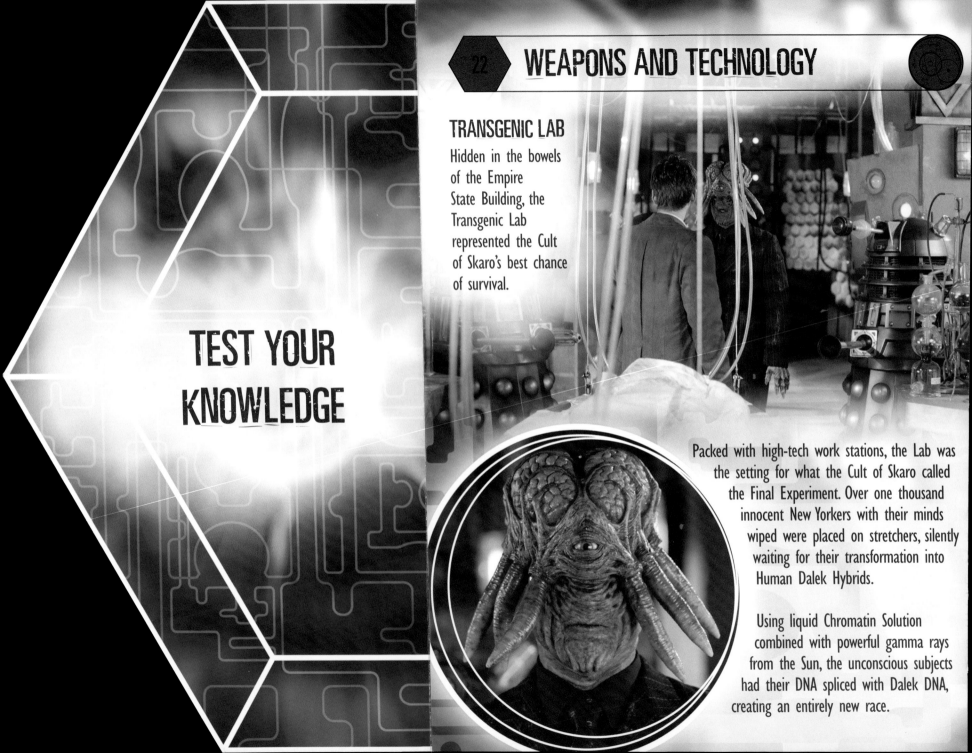

TRANSGENIC LAB

Hidden in the bowels of the Empire State Building, the Transgenic Lab represented the Cult of Skaro's best chance of survival.

TEST YOUR KNOWLEDGE

Packed with high-tech work stations, the Lab was the setting for what the Cult of Skaro called the Final Experiment. Over one thousand innocent New Yorkers with their minds wiped were placed on stretchers, silently waiting for their transformation into Human Dalek Hybrids.

Using liquid Chromatin Solution combined with powerful gamma rays from the Sun, the unconscious subjects had their DNA spliced with Dalek DNA, creating an entirely new race.

TEMPORAL SHIFT

In addition to their superior weaponry and powerful force field, the Daleks in the Cult of Skaro can also travel in time using a Temporal Shift. In an emergency, this can be used as a means of escape. But an Emergency Temporal Shift is unpredictable as the Dalek is unable to set specific coordinates.

When the Cult of Skaro escaped from the Battle of Canary Wharf, they ended up in New York in 1930. Dalek Caan again used an Emergency Temporal Shift to escape from the Doctor in New York — and he could have arrived at any point in Earth's history!

THE VOID SHIP AND THE GENESIS ARK

With the Great Time War between the Daleks and the Time Lords raging around them, the Cult of Skaro boarded a Void Ship and hid unnoticed in the space between dimensions.

They took with them an amazing piece of technology called the Genesis Ark. This Ark was actually a prison created by the Time Lords. Although it didn't appear to be very big, it was dimensionally transcendental, just like the TARDIS. It was much bigger on the inside and contained thousands of captured Daleks.

1. WHERE DID THE CULT OF SKARO
CONDUCT THE FINAL EXPERIMENT?
A. The Transgenic Lab
B. New Jersey
C. Their home planet of Skaro

2. WHAT WAS THE NAME OF THE LIQUID
USED TO CREATE HUMAN DALEKS?
A. Gamma Solution
B. Chromatin Solution
C. Washing-up liquid

3. HOW CAN THE CULT OF SKARO
ESCAPE FROM DANGER?
A. By hiding behind the sofa
B. By wearing a disguise
C. By operating an Emergency
Temporal Shift

4. WHERE DID THE CULT HIDE
WHEN THEY ESCAPED
THE TIME WAR?
A. Under the sea
B. Between dimensions
C. A parallel world

5. WHICH TIME LORD CREATION WAS
STOLEN BY THE CULT OF SKARO?
A. The Genesis Ark
B. Noah's Ark
C. The Ark in Space

MIND-READING

The best way to think
as your enemy does is to
read their thoughts! The Cult
of Skaro Daleks are capable of
extracting human brainwaves.

They can also initiate an Intelligence
Scan — something that came in very
handy when deciding who would become a
Pig Slave and who would become a Human
Dalek. Only the cleverest humans were considered
worthy of having their DNA spliced with the Daleks.

TEST YOUR KNOWLEDGE

THE BATTLE OF CANARY WHARF

The Doctor thought that the Daleks had all been destroyed in the Great Time War - apart from the one which fell to Earth, that he met in Van Statten's museum. When the Cybermen came through to Earth from a parallel world, they were joined by a strange sphere. The sphere contained the four Daleks of the Cult of Skaro and the Genesis Ark. The Cult had hidden in the Void between universes, waiting for the right time to open the Ark and release the army of Daleks imprisoned inside.

Both the Daleks and the
Cybermen thought the
Earth should be theirs.
The Cybermen suggested
an alliance of their
forces, together they
could upgrade the
whole universe. But
the Cult of Skaro
knew the Cybermen
were an inferior
species and chose to
destroy them instead.
The Doctor defeated
all of them by sending
them back into the Void.
Only the Cult of Skaro
managed to escape.

DALEKS IN MANHATTAN

Powerless after escaping the battle, the Cult of Skaro materialized in 1930's New York. With the help of an army of Pig Slaves, the last of the Daleks collected as many people as possible to take part in the Final Experiment - making a new race of Human Daleks.

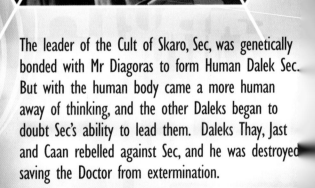

The leader of the Cult of Skaro, Sec, was genetically bonded with Mr Diagoras to form Human Dalek Sec. But with the human body came a more human away of thinking, and the other Daleks began to doubt Sec's ability to lead them. Daleks Thay, Jast and Caan rebelled against Sec, and he was destroyed saving the Doctor from extermination.

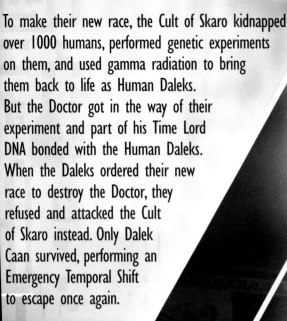

To make their new race, the Cult of Skaro kidnapped over 1000 humans, performed genetic experiments on them, and used gamma radiation to bring them back to life as Human Daleks. But the Doctor got in the way of their experiment and part of his Time Lord DNA bonded with the Human Daleks. When the Daleks ordered their new race to destroy the Doctor, they refused and attacked the Cult of Skaro instead. Only Dalek Caan survived, performing an Emergency Temporal Shift to escape once again.

He's out there somewhere — the last member of the Cult of Skaro - hiding in time and space, ready to wreak his revenge on the Doctor and anyone foolish enough to stand in his way.

1. WHERE WAS THE FIRST DALEK THAT THE DOCTOR MET AFTER THE GREAT TIME WAR?
A. Van Statten's museum
B. The Dalek planet, Skaro
C. Shopping in the supermarket

2. WHAT DID THE CULT OF SKARO RELEASE FROM THE GENESIS ARK?
A. The Genesis Device
B. A Void Ship
C. An army of Daleks

3. WHAT ANIMAL DO THE DALEK SLAVES LOOK LIKE?
A. Bears
B. Kangaroos
C. Pigs

4. HOW MANY HUMANS DID THE CULT KIDNAP?
A. More than 10
B. Over 1,000
C. Almost 10,000

5. WHOSE DNA GOT MIXED UP WITH THE HUMAN DALEKS?
A. Martha's
B. Tallulah's
C. The Doctor's

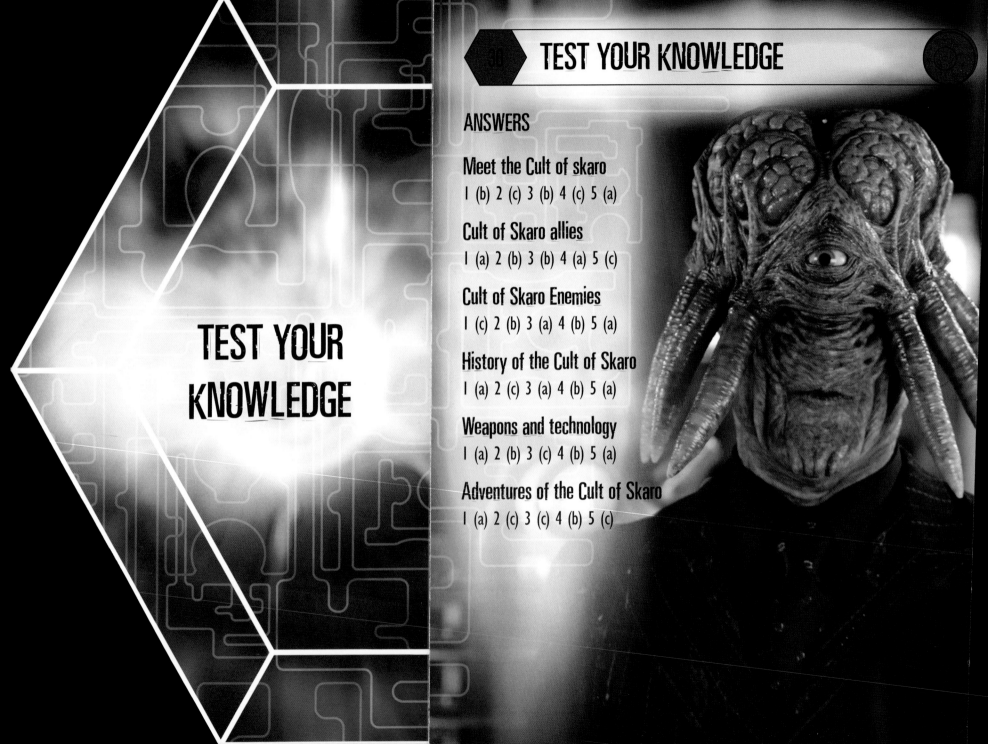

TEST YOUR KNOWLEDGE

ANSWERS

Meet the Cult of skaro
1 (b) 2 (c) 3 (b) 4 (c) 5 (a)

Cult of Skaro allies
1 (a) 2 (b) 3 (b) 4 (a) 5 (c)

Cult of Skaro Enemies
1 (c) 2 (b) 3 (a) 4 (b) 5 (a)

History of the Cult of Skaro
1 (a) 2 (c) 3 (a) 4 (b) 5 (a)

Weapons and technology
1 (a) 2 (b) 3 (c) 4 (b) 5 (a)

Adventures of the Cult of Skaro
1 (a) 2 (c) 3 (c) 4 (b) 5 (c)

BIRTH OF A LEGEND

Firelight flickered across the bronze dome of the Dalek Commander. Explosions were reflected on its burnished casing as it surveyed the scene below. The entire power complex was on fire – a massive city on stilts high above the jungle, and the source for the power that controlled all Mechonoid operations on Magella. This was the final stronghold of the Mechonoid resistance.

In the skies above the burning complex, a massive space saucer waited in geostationary orbit, its scanners recording every moment of the battle below. It recorded the Dalek units moving through the buildings, the robotic life signs of the Mechonoids – winking out one by one – and the exact points of fire and explosion, detonation and death. The information would be analysed and any useful conclusions fed back into the Dalek battle computers for future campaigns.

The Dalek Commander could have stayed on the saucer, plugged directly into the Military Computer and absorbing every tiny piece of data as it came in. But the Commander of the Seventh

Incursion Squad preferred to watch from close by. It believed it could react more quickly to changes on the battlefront if it could observe them close up and at first hand. With three other Daleks it was on a ridge half way up the mountain that overshadowed the mighty city, looking down at the devastation.

Smoke drifted across the valley and the Daleks watching switched frequencies on their visual scanners to see through it. Their listening scanners picked up and monitored the sounds of the explosions, the robotic croaks of the retreating Mechonoids, the constant cry of 'Exterminate!'

The Commander watched as a Dalek appeared out of the fires below. It rose majestically towards the vantage point where the Commander was keeping watch. The Dalek's casing was scarred and scorched from Mechonoid flame guns, but intact.

'Report,' ordered the Commander as the Dalek arrived.

'Unit Nine reports that Mechonoids are regrouping in the

main reactor area. They

may be preparing to mount

a counteroffensive against

Dalek forces.'

　　　Another Dalek

glided forward from the

small group gathered

behind the Commander.

'Main Saucer confirms

Unit Nine's analysis.

Military Computer has

determined the best

strategy is to advance

all units immediately

into reactor area.'

The Commander's dome swung round and its eye stalk fixed on the Dalek that had spoken. 'Have scanners checked for plasmic activity?'

'Negative. Mechonoids would not deploy plasmic explosives so close to their main reactors.'

The Commander's eye stalk did not waver. 'Check for deployment of plasmic explosives. The Mechonoids may be preparing to destroy the reactors completely and destroy all Dalek forces within the main city complex.'

'Plasmic signature detected,' the reporting Dalek confirmed. 'The Mechonoids will detonate.' Its voice rose in pitch as it received further data. 'Priming sequence has begun. Detonation will follow in approximately fifty rels.'

The commander turned back to the Dalek hovering in front of them, the Daleks from the battleground below. 'Order all Dalek units to disengage and retreat to outer city perimeter. Move!' The Dalek zoomed off, back into the smoke and fire and death.

'Analsysis suggests total area of devastation will extend beyond the city and destroy all Dalek forces currently operating on Magella,' the Dalek in touch with the saucer reported. 'Detonation in forty rels.'

The Commander turned. 'Order space saucer to target main reactors with thronic missiles. Fire in thirty rels.'

'I obey.'

'Should we evacuate?' another Dalek asked. The Commander did not reply.

Far below, Daleks were emerging from the burning buildings and regrouping round the edge of the city. Where there had once been a heavily fortified security wall, now only a blacked, ragged edge marked where the wall and gun emplacements had been.

Two beams of light streaked down through the sky and focused on the main reactor building standing almost intact in the middle of the devastation. The thronic aura beam would act as a guide for the missiles that were already on their way.

Moments later, the main reactor building exploded in a crimson flower of flame. The whole city shook, the heart torn out of it. A gaping, smoking hole lay in the centre of the city complex. But the structure round the edges remained intact.

'Thronic missiles enhanced and focused plasmic detonation,' the Dalek Commander observed above the rumble of continuing explosions. 'Reactors have been completely vaporized and blast damage is minimal.'

'Battlefield commander reports no loss to Dalek forces. All Mechonoids now exterminated.'

The Commander swung round. If there was a trace of satisfaction in its voice, it was almost impossible to detect. 'The Mechonoids gave us the means to destroy them. Dalek strategy remains supreme. The Daleks will conquer the universe!'

'Data from Military Computers has been relayed to Dalek Central Control,' a Dalek reported to the Commander. 'You are ordered to report to Skaro immediately.'

'All Daleks return to ship,' the Commander ordered. 'Compute a course to Skaro.'

'Negative. Incursion Squad Seven is ordered to complete operations here.' The Dalek glided forward, its eye stalk level with its Commander's. 'I will assume command of all operations on this planet. The order to return to Skaro has the Emperor's ident codes, and relates only to you.'

The enormous Throne Room at the centre of the Dalek City on Skaro echoed with the heartbeat-like throb of Dalek systems. The room was so big it didn't seem to have walls – just shadows where the light ran out and darkness took over.

A black-domed Imperial Guard led the Commander to the centre of the room, where three other Daleks were already waiting. The Commander quickly scanned their identification codes. One of them was the Commandant of Station Alpha – the most secret Dalek research facility. The second was an Attack Squad Leader in the Thirtieth Assault Group. The third Dalek was Force Leader of the Outer Rim Defensive Batallion.

All four Daleks were dwarfed by the enormous shape of the Emperor itself. A massive eye stalk swung across as the Emperor examined the Daleks brought before it. Black-domed Imperial Guard Daleks withdrew into the shadows.

The Emperor's voice was like a hundred Daleks all speaking

at once, echoing round the chamber as it addressed them. 'You have been called here for a purpose. Your mission is vital to the survival of our race. I put the future of the Daleks in your control.'

'You are our Emperor,' the Commander replied. 'We exist to serve. We have the capacity to execute any orders we are given.'

'More than that!' the Emperor said. 'You four have demonstrated abilities above and beyond the simple execution of orders. You have been successful in every endeavour. You have used...' The Emperor paused, before finishing: 'Initiative.'

All four Daleks eye stalks dipped slightly, before the Emperor continued: 'And that is good.'

The Commander's dome turned as it surveyed the other three Daleks. They seemed equally puzzled, looking at each other, then back at the Emperor.

'It is not the Dalek way to question,' the Emperor intoned. 'Yet I do question.' Its eye swung to look at each of the four Daleks in turn.

'Our strategy computers and assessment engines predict that there is a war coming. An ancient Enemy that may be a match even for the Daleks.'

'No one can oppose the Daleks,' the Force Leader rasped.

'Silence!' the Emperor commanded. 'The war will come. It will rage throughout all time and all space. It will take our every resource, our every stratagem, just to survive.'

'Daleks should be victorious,' the Commander said.

'Agreed. But to be sure of victory, we must employ new methods. We must question what it is to be Dalek.'

'No enemy can be so dangerous,' the Dalek from Station Alpha said. 'Unless…' It's voice stopped abruptly, dome lights dimmed.

The unspoken name of the great enemy hung in the chamber.

'What must we do?' the Commander asked at last.

'You four have been brought here to form a new weapon. You are that weapon. You will be reconditioned to allow you to think as no Dalek has ever been able to think. You will think like the enemy. You will become like the enemy. You will dare to plan and act in ways that no other Dalek would countenance. Even your Emperor.' The lights seemed to dim in the room as the Emperor spoke. 'You will be the Cult of Skaro.'

'The Cult of Skaro,' the Daleks intoned in unison.

'You will be our greatest weapon,' the Emperor went on. 'And you will be our greatest secret. A legend, a myth, a rumour to strike fear into the hearts of the Enemy. And to demonstrate how far the Daleks will go for victory – you will have names.'

Despite itself, the Commander moved backwards in surprise and trepidation.

The Emperor's eye took in each Dalek in turn. 'You will be Thay. You are Caan. You are Dalek Jast…' The eye stopped at last at the Commander. 'You will lead the Cult of Skaro,' the Emperor said. 'As Dalek Sec. And you will all be enhanced and improved. No Daleks have ever been more powerful, or more vital to our survival. Go now, and begin the great task.'

The four Daleks swept out, black-domed Imperial Guards leading them to the Weapons Factory where they would be fitted with the latest armour and weaponry.

Dalek Sec was led through to a special experimental laboratory at the back of the Weapons Factory.

'The Emperor has ordered that you be given a new casing,' a Dalek scientist explained. 'We have it prepared. Unseal your casing.'

The bronzed shell that protected Dalek Sec split open down the front, panels swinging away to reveal the grotesque Dalek creature inside. Slowly, gently – almost reverently – the creature was lifted out of the casing. A new casing of highly-polished black metal was moved into position and the creature placed inside. With a hiss of powerful hydraulics, the new casing swung shut.

'This casing is made from an enhanced form of Dalekanium, called Metalert,' the scientist explained.

Sec swung slowly round, checking the movement and sensor capabilities of the new casing.

'How is Metalert better than Dalekanium?' Sec demanded. 'Why are not all Daleks made from Metalert?'

'The casing is infused with very rare materials,' the scientist said. 'It is reinforced with flidor gold and sap from the extinct Arkellis flower. You are a Dalek like no other.'

Dalek Sec did not answer. It knew the scientist was right. Sec glided majestically from the Weapons Factory, three other Daleks – Thay, Caan, and Jast – moving into position behind Sec. Together they headed for a new section of the Dalek City.

A special area where no other Daleks would ever go.

The place where they would begin their awesome mission: The secret Strategy Chambers of the Cult of Skaro.

DOCTOR · WHO

OTHER GREAT FILES TO COLLECT